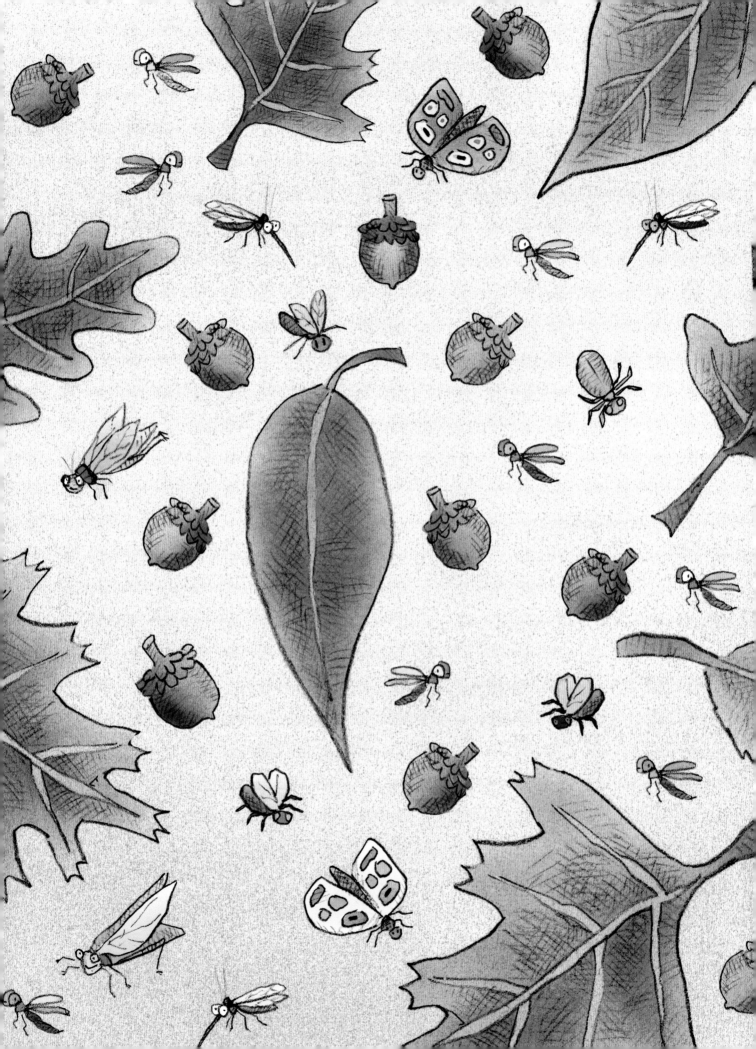

Good Night, Bat! Good Morning, Squirrel!

BY PAUL MEISEL

BOYDS MILLS PRESS
AN IMPRINT OF HIGHLIGHTS
Honesdale, Pennsylvania

For Cheryl, who first thought
Bat and Squirrel could be friends

Text and illustrations copyright © 2016 by Paul Meisel
All rights reserved.
For information about permission to reproduce selections from this book,
contact permissions@highlights.com.

Boyds Mills Press
An Imprint of Highlights
815 Church Street
Honesdale, Pennsylvania 18431

Printed in China
ISBN: 978-1-62979-495-2
Library of Congress Control Number: 2015958504

First edition
Production by Sue Cole
The text of this book is set in Futuramano.
The illustrations are done in charcoal and litho crayon on strathmore paper, then digitally colored.
10 9 8 7 6 5 4 3 2 1

Bat needed a new home.

"I lost my home. Can I stay with you?" said Bat.

"Sorry. We already have too many bats,"
the old bat said.

"I lost my home. Can I live here?" said Bat.
"Yes, but I might eat you," said the fox.
"No, thank you," said Bat.

"I lost my home. Can I share yours?" asked Bat.
"No way. Bats are stinky. Please go away,"
said the skunk.

Bat searched high.

Bat searched low.

And Bat searched
everywhere in between.

Then he spotted something.

The clump of leaves and
sticks had a small opening
with a cozy home inside.

Bat could even hang from one
of the twigs at bedtime.

Perfect, thought Bat. Bat gathered bugs
for a snack for later. Then he hopped up
on a twig and fell fast asleep.

Squirrel was dreaming of nuts.

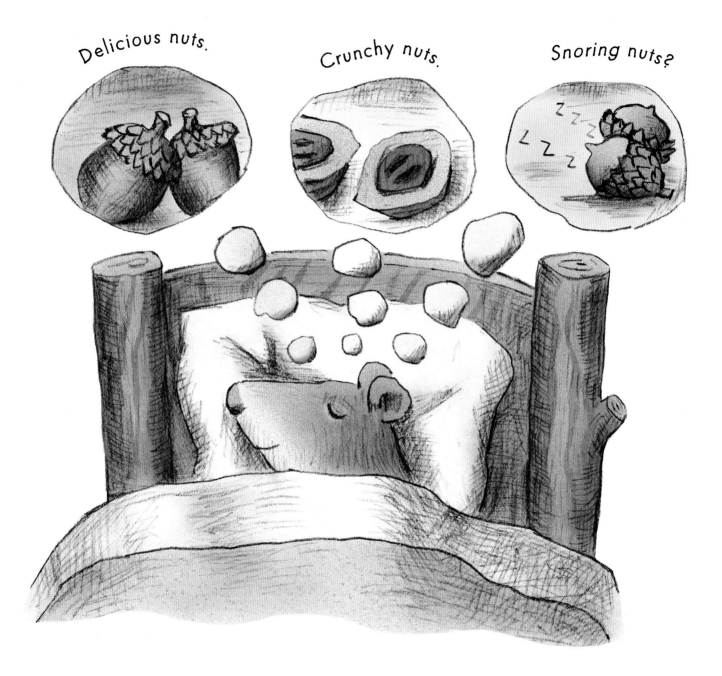

Delicious nuts.

Crunchy nuts.

Snoring nuts?

When Squirrel woke up, she was startled to discover a bat sleeping upside down.

"Excuse me! This is MY home," Squirrel said to Bat.

Zzzz

Squirrel shook Bat.
"I'm going out to hide
acorns. Please leave
before I get back."

But Squirrel had a feeling that Bat wasn't listening.
To be on the safe side, Squirrel left a note.

At dusk, Bat woke up
and found the note.

Oh, Squirrel doesn't like bugs on her bed, thought Bat.

He piled the bugs in a corner, wrote Squirrel a polite reply, and then took off for bug hunting.

Sorry about
the bugs!
See you later!
Bat ☺

Squirrel came home a little while later,
ready for a good night's sleep.
See you later? she thought. We'll see
about that!

Before climbing into bed, she hung
a new note outside near the opening.

Hunting mosquitoes, hoppers, and stinkbugs all night made Bat tired. He couldn't wait to curl up on his twig.

When he got back to Squirrel's house, he saw the new note.

What a nice friend, thought Bat.
He wrote back to Squirrel.

"Again?!" said Squirrel
when Bat's snoring woke her up.
Before she left for another
busy day, she wrote her
most forceful note yet.

Bat woke up. He stretched. Squirrel's
latest note was hard to miss. Bat smiled
when he read it. *OK*, he thought.

In the moonlight, Bat added
more leaves to Squirrel's house.
It nearly doubled in size.
Bat was exhausted after the
long night of work. Before he
fell asleep, he wrote to Squirrel.

I leaved your house. Hope you like it! Bat :)

Huh? thought Squirrel when she read the new note. *This bat is batty!*

Before she left the snoring bat
to find nuts, Squirrel thought she
would write one very last note.

Outside, she noticed all the new leaves.
That's pretty nice, thought Squirrel.

Bat woke up at sunset.

He didn't see Squirrel in her bed.

"SKI-ram? A-de-OS? Good-bye?" read Bat.

"I wonder why Squirrel left?" Bat flew off
to find bugs.

Meanwhile, Squirrel sat on a stump. She was sure her last note made Bat leave.

She started to miss him. *He did fix up my house,* thought Squirrel. *And he writes such nice notes.*

While catching bugs, Bat thought about how lonely it would be without Squirrel.

He started to miss Squirrel.

Bat flew back just as Squirrel came home late.

"You didn't leave!" Squirrel shouted happily.

"You didn't either!" shouted Bat.

"Want to come inside? I'll teach you my favorite game," said Squirrel.

"Sure!" said Bat.

Bat and Squirrel played tic-tac-toe until sunrise.

"That was fun. I'm sleepy." Bat yawned
as he hopped up on his stick.
"Good night, Bat!" said Squirrel.
"Good morning, Squirrel!" said Bat.

"See you later," said Squirrel.
But Squirrel had a feeling that Bat wasn't listening.

So Squirrel left one very, very last note.